Special Lifestyles and Customs

U0103560

商務印書館（香港）有限公司
http://www.commercialpress.com.hk

CENGAGE
Learning™

Australia • Brazil • Japan • Korea • Mexico • Singapore • Spain • United Kingdom • United States

Special Lifestyles and Customs 獨特生活風情

Main English text © 2010 Heinle, Cengage Learning
English footnotes © 2010 Heinle, Cengage Learning and The Commercial Press (H.K.) Ltd.
Chinese text © 2010 The Commercial Press (H.K.) Ltd.

香港特別版由Heinle, a part of Cengage Learning 及商務印書館（香港）有限公司聯合出版。
This special Hong Kong edition is co-published by Heinle, a part of Cengage Learning, and The Commercial Press (H.K.) Ltd.

Director of Content Development:
Anita Raducanu
Series Editor: Rob Waring
Editorial Manager: Bryan Fletcher

Associate Development Editors:
Victoria Forrester, Catherine McCue
責任編輯：黃家麗

出版：

商務印書館（香港）有限公司
香港筲箕灣耀興道3號東滙廣場8樓

Cengage Learning
Units 808-810, 8th floor,
Tins Enterprises Centre,
777 Lai Chi Kok Road, Cheung Sha Wan,
Kowloon, Hong Kong

網址：http://www.commercialpress.com.hk

http://www.cengageasia.com

發行：香港聯合書刊物流有限公司
　　　香港新界大埔汀麗路36號中華商務
　　　印刷大廈3字樓

印刷：中華商務彩色印刷有限公司
版次：2010年7月 第1版第1次印刷

ISBN: 978-962-07-1909-7 (Commercial Press)
ISBN: 978-1-111-35144-1 (Cengage Learning)

出版說明

本館一向倡導優質閱讀，近年連續推出以 "Q" 為標誌的優質英語學習系列(*Quality English Learning*)，其中《Black Cat 優質英語階梯閱讀》，讀者反應令人鼓舞，先後共推出超過60本。

為進一步推動閱讀，本館引入Cengage 出版之*Footprint Library*，使用*National Geographic*的圖像及語料，編成百科英語階梯閱讀系列，有別於Black Cat 古典文學閱讀，透過現代真實題材，百科英語語境能幫助讀者認識今日的世界各事各物，擴闊視野，提高認識及表達英語的能力。

本系列屬non-fiction (非虛構故事類)讀本，結合閱讀、視像和聽力三種學習功能，是一套三合一多媒介讀本，每本書的英文文章以headwords寫成，headwords 選收自以下數據庫的語料：*Collins Cobuild The Bank of English*、*British National Corpus* 及 *BYU Corpus of American English* 等，並配上精彩照片，另加一張video/audio 兩用DVD。編排由淺入深，按級提升，只要讀者堅持學習，必能有效提高英語溝通能力。

商務印書館(香港)有限公司

編輯部

使用説明

百科英語階梯閱讀分六級，共十六本書，是彩色有影有聲書，每本有英語文章供閱讀，根據數據庫如 *Collins Cobuild The Bank of English*、*British National Corpus* 及 *BYU Corpus of American English* 選收常用字詞編寫，配彩色照片及一張video/audio兩用DVD，結合閱讀、聆聽、視像三種學習方式。

讀者可使用本書：

 學習新詞彙，並透過延伸閱讀(Expansion Reading)練習速讀技巧

 聆聽錄音提高聽力，模仿標準英語讀音

 看短片做練習，以提升綜合理解能力

Grammar Focus解釋語法重點，後附練習題，供讀者即時複習所學，書內其他練習題，有助讀者掌握學習技巧如 scanning, prediction, summarising, identifying the main idea

中英對照生詞表設於書後，既不影響讀者閱讀正文，又具備參考作用

Contents 目錄

The CD-ROM contains a video and full recording of the text

CD-ROM *包括短片和錄音*

Words to Know

This story is set on the Orient Express, a train that travels through seven countries in Europe to go from Paris, France, over the Alps to Istanbul, Turkey.

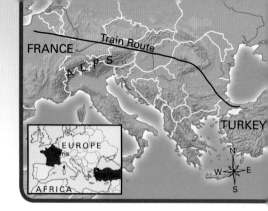

 The Orient Express. Read the paragraph. Then match each word or phrase with the correct definition.

The legendary Orient Express became well known in a bygone era as it carried Europe's wealthy and royal passengers between France and Turkey. With its luxurious decor, the Orient Express evokes images of elegance, romance, and mystery. While the routes may be different now, passengers aboard this luxury train can still be pampered with delicious, first-class cuisine and excellent service as they travel through the varied terrain of Europe.

1. bygone era _____   **a.** the natural features of land; the landscape

2. royal _____   **b.** the art and science of cooking

3. decor _____   **c.** bring out a feeling or thought

4. evoke _____   **d.** the decorative environment of a place

5. romance _____   **e.** spoil; take more care of than is necessary

6. pamper _____   **f.** a period of time in the past

7. cuisine _____   **g.** related to or appropriate for a king or queen

8. terrain _____   **h.** a feeling of excitement, adventure, and happiness

The Orient Express

B **Working on a Legend.** Read the definitions of the types of jobs found on the Orient Express. Then label the pictures with the correct <u>underlined</u> words.

A <u>barman</u> serves drinks at a bar.
A <u>cabin steward</u> cleans and tidies the cabins on the train.
The <u>chef</u> is a skilled cook, especially the main cook in a restaurant.
The <u>maitre d'</u> is in charge of a restaurant and its waiters and waitresses.

1. _____

2. _____

3. _____

4. _____

Working on the Orient Express is a tremendous opportunity for many people.

With its famous **boulevards**,[1] historic buildings, and elegant and relaxed atmosphere, Paris is a city that the whole world often associates with romance. Today, though, at one of Paris' grand train stations, people are not looking for love in the **literal sense**,[2] but romance of another kind, from another time. They want to go back to an age when simply getting somewhere was an adventure, a time when Paris was the departure point for the world's most famous train: the Orient Express.

'Good Morning. How are you?' says an American tourist as he approaches a unique ticket desk that sits in front of a long, peculiar train. The train's deep colour, classic design, and antique style stand out against its modern-looking surroundings. The tourist is checking in to board the Orient Express, which was once known as 'the Train of Kings and the King of Trains'. In every detail, the Orient Express evokes the elegant images of a golden age: the beautiful decor and **furnishings**,[3] the shiny wood panelling, the fine china and silver that cover the dining tables, and of course, the service. When it began operating at the turn of the 20th century, the train carried members of Europe's royal families and rich business leaders from Paris to Constantinople or Istanbul as the Turkish city is now called. These days, this luxurious train still makes the journey from Paris across Europe to Istanbul, but it does it just once a year – and it's a journey some wait a lifetime to take.

---

[1] **boulevard:** wide street, usually lined with trees; an avenue
[2] **literal sense:** the original basic meaning of a word
[3] **furnishings:** furniture, window and floor coverings, and other objects for homes and offices

Skim for Gist

Read through the entire passage quickly to answer the questions.

1. What is the reading basically about?

2. Which two groups of people related to the Orient Express are mentioned in the reading?

As the train commences its travels in Paris, passengers settle in for a six-day journey through seven countries across the continent of Europe. It may be a long physical journey, but it's more than that – it's also a voyage into the passengers' own imaginations. Eli, a passenger on this trip, explains that for him it's all about a journey into the past, into history. 'What I really wanted to get out of the Orient Express was the feeling of going into – [or] stepping into – a time machine. The idea that I could go back to a bygone era, not just any time, but a time before I was even born and experience what it would have been like.'

For most of the 85 passengers on the run from France to Turkey, the **pampering**[1] and luxury of this famous voyage are a once-in-a-lifetime treat. Passenger Bill Hummel is typical of many passengers in that he and his wife are celebrating something special. 'It has many meanings for us,' he says. 'My wife had her sixtieth birthday in June and our twenty-fifth wedding anniversary was the twentieth of August.'

---

[1]**pamper:** to make sb feel very comfortable

Passengers come from all parts of the world and many are taking this special trip because they're celebrating a special or private occasion. However, there is one thing that everyone aboard the train seems to have in common: a desire to somehow recapture a lost age and to live an experience that has caught even the **literary**[1] imagination. Karen Prothero, marketing director of the Orient Express explains: 'There's a huge fascination for the train and then of course **Agatha Christie**[2] wrote that famous book, "Murder on the Orient Express", which has also helped so much to make it such a famous name.'

The Orient Express hasn't continuously operated since the route was first established so long ago, though. In the mid-1940s, after World War ll, the possibility of taking an aeroplane to travel to foreign countries, as well as the rise of the **Iron Curtain**[3] between the East and West, made this type of luxury travel by train impractical. The Orient Express consequently **suspended**[4] its service until 1997 when it restarted the Paris to Istanbul route.

---

[1]**literary:** related to literature and writing
[2]**Agatha Christie:** (1890–1976) an English crime author, best known for her detective novels
[3]**Iron Curtain:** the political and philosophical barriers or separation between Communist countries and democracies that began after World War II and ended in 1989 with the fall of the Berlin Wall
[4]**suspend:** to stop sth for a short time

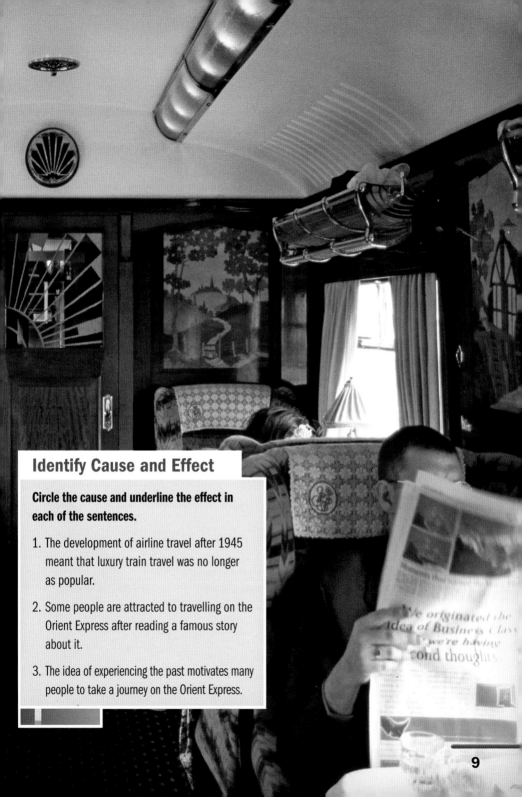

Identify Cause and Effect

Circle the cause and underline the effect in each of the sentences.

1. The development of airline travel after 1945 meant that luxury train travel was no longer as popular.

2. Some people are attracted to travelling on the Orient Express after reading a famous story about it.

3. The idea of experiencing the past motivates many people to take a journey on the Orient Express.

For many people, the attraction of the Paris to Istanbul journey is completely irresistible and experiencing it is something that they've dreamed about for ages. It's easy to entertain thoughts of taking a long, lazy journey surrounded by magnificent mountain scenery, all while being pampered with service worthy of kings, complete with proper English afternoon tea delivered to one's **travel compartment**.[1]

University lecturer Robert Franklin explains his motivation for making the trip across Europe. 'I've always been a lover of travel,' he says, 'and always [been] in search of particularly **exotic**[2] and unusual travel **venues**.[3] The history, the **terrain**[4] that we are travelling, I mean it's just **soaked with**[5] the blood of saints and warriors and **visionaries**.[6] For me, as a teacher and as a writer, it's really pretty inspiring.'

---

[1]**travel compartment:** the small area on a train or ship in which one journeys
[2]**exotic:** having a strange beauty, originating in a foreign country
[3]**venue:** location; setting or scene
[4]**terrain:** an area of land that has a special physical feature
[5]**soaked with:** influenced by
[6]**visionaries:** people who planned imaginatively and wisely for the future

As it winds through the magnificent scenery of the Alps, the Orient Express crosses a countryside that consistently displays its finest. Passengers on the train are expected to do no less. As night falls, they begin to prepare for dinner, which on the Orient Express is a formal affair. Passengers must wear their best **attire**,[1] including formal evening suits and dresses. The elegant meals often include fine wines, several courses, and soft music to accompany the dining experience, all adding to the sense that the trip is more than just a train journey. It is a trip where the journey itself is the destination. The idea isn't really to simply arrive somewhere, it's to have an incredible experience along the way – and that includes dining in style. The dinner is always **superb**[2] and the atmosphere consistently romantic.

As the evening grows late, the Orient Express rolls along into the night, continuing to make the dreams and wishes of its passengers come true. 'It has been a dream for a long time to participate in this little bit of history,' says Robert Franklin. 'It's hard to imagine a more extraordinary and romantic journey than to travel from Paris to Istanbul on the Orient Express.'

---

[1] **attire:** clothing; dress
[2] **superb:** excellent

The next day, while the morning mist **hangs around**[1] the sleepy fields of Europe, the world's most famous train comes alive. As the Orient Express rolls across eastern Austria, window shades are opened, surfaces are polished until they shine, and breakfast is brought to those who choose not to come to the dining car. It all happens quickly, smoothly, and seemingly effortlessly – almost as if by magic.

Making the huge and expensive train operate smoothly isn't magic. Breakfast doesn't appear without staff to prepare it and a train such as this needs top-class employees. The work on the train has been done by an army of well-trained staff for years. It seems that working on a legend has its rewards. As the team of breakfast waiters rushes to prepare for the morning diners, one can see them smiling as they move through the luxurious furnishings. A cabin steward in charge of making sure that the sleeping cabins are perfectly maintained describes his thoughts about the train. '[It's] a wonderful, wonderful hotel on wheels,' he reports.

---

[1]**hang around:** to float or hover in the air

The staff of the Orient Express knows all about providing first-class service since most of them have also worked in Europe's finest hotels and restaurants. However, when they join the train, they soon find that there are some significant differences between working in a hotel in a city, and working on this 'hotel on wheels'. One barman talks about the main differences and how they affect him and his work practices. 'Working on a train is very different,' he comments, 'because you have the scenery which is always changing. In an operational way it's also very different from working in a hotel, so you have to be very well organised.' One can imagine the planning that must be involved for a barman. He must be able to prepare for a trip during which every person expects world-class service but for which there are no alternative resources for supplies, staff, or working conditions.

There are certainly challenges unique to running a five-star hotel on wheels over a long period of time. These days, the six-day journey through seven countries happens only once every 12 months, but planning for it takes an entire year. Maintaining the proper amount of goods, or stock, on the train is essential. 'We move all the time,' says the **maitre d'**.[1] 'The train is not like a new train. It wasn't built yesterday, as you know, and then we have limited stock of everything, so we have to try to make it last.' The barman agrees that planning in advance is important, so that they don't run out of food or drinks. 'And it's not easy,' he explains with a smile. 'Instead of a hotel, [where] if you're missing something you just go down to the canteen and get it, it's a bit different on the train.' These barmen can't **pop out**[2] for a specific ingredient; they're only able to work with what is available to them on the train – and that's limited by availability, space, and capacity to be preserved.

---

[1]**maitre d':** sb who is in charge of waiters and waitresses in a restaurant
[2]**pop out:** to go out and come back quickly

In addition to the annual Paris to Istanbul run, the Orient Express has offered a regular seasonal service between Venice and London for over 20 years. Still, the staff seem to learn something new on every journey and the organisation and planning are constantly improving. One of the unusual problems they must continuously face is trying to stay on their feet while creating world class cuisine since the movement of the train can be problematic for the staff. Chef Christian Bodiguel stands in his tiny kitchen and explains just how hard it is for him to work because the train's movement causes everything – including him and his assistant chef – to swing from side to side. 'It's very difficult because [as] you can see it's mov[ing] now. For me it's very difficult because we have a small kitchen and it's moving, moving, moving.' It's very difficult for the chef and his staff to safely cut and prepare vegetables or cook soups and other liquids in a constantly shifting kitchen.

The situation is no different for the number of barmen and waiters that must be able to offer food and drinks to their high-class, well-dressed passengers without spilling a drop. While it is challenging, for some the movement of the train actually can help with the work. When asked if working on a train is difficult, one barman replies, 'Ah, it is, but we're used to it, especially working out on the tables.' He then goes on to add, 'The movement … it keeps you busy. It keeps you very concentrated actually. It's relaxing sometimes.'

A chef working on the
Orient Express usually
faces unusual problems.

The service on the train must consistently meet a high standard of service and the train's general manager Claude Gianella can most probably be credited for that. He explains that for him, service has been the most important aspect of his work on the Orient Express for the past 20 years. 'Without being **presumptuous**,'[1] he reports, 'it has been my main objective for those twenty years to keep the highest possible level of service on what is, after all, a train.'

For many in the high-class service industry, the secret of excellent service is to make it all look effortless. To gain this appearance, much of the work on the train is done behind the scenes where the guests can't see the staff hard at work. At various stops along the route, for example, food is loaded onto the train. Several different types of **produce**[2] come on board at these times, from fresh fruit to freshly caught fish packed in ice. It all has to happen quickly and **discreetly**[3] so that the food remains under the best possible conditions and the passengers don't see the action. The kitchens are completely restocked within minutes to meet these demands and to keep the train right on track.

---

[1] **presumptuous:** self-important; showing a lack of respect by doing things not normally permitted
[2] **produce:** fruit, vegetables, and other things that farmers grow
[3] **discreetly:** carefully and politely, without people knowing about what you are doing

Infer Meaning

1. What does the writer mean by 'behind the scenes'?

2. What does the writer mean by saying they need to 'keep the train right on track'?

Travelling through seven countries also involves occasional border challenges as well as some changes that must happen as the Orient Express approaches each border. In each country the Orient Express takes on a new **locomotive**[1] engine and engineer in order to ensure passengers' safety and that the train runs smoothly. But while the locomotive and engineer change, the rest of the staff on each trip stays the same throughout the journey – and often throughout the years, it seems.

The cabin steward who described the train as a 'wonderful hotel on wheels' is now in his fourth season with the train, but others have worked on the Orient Express for much longer. 'I've been on the Orient Express for thirteen years now,' says the maitre d'. Chef Bodiguel has worked even longer: 'Fifteen years on board,' he says. 'Fifteen years I [have] work[ed] here.'

---

[1]**locomotive:** a large railway vehicle with an engine

It's clear that once someone starts working aboard the Orient Express, it's often difficult for them to consider doing anything else. It's obvious that the barman is very proud of the work he does when he sums up the pleasures of working on the Orient Express: 'It's unique. It is. When you go into a train station, the people outside are looking at the train and you can sort of imagine them thinking how much they'd like to be on that train and you're on it. I mean you're working on it, which is even better. I mean, it's something very special.'

The people who travel and work on the Orient Express have a window-seat view of Europe passing before their eyes and a close up of a bygone era surrounding them. When it comes to romance and adventure while travelling in style, it seems that none of the modern travel options of today can come close to a romantic ride on the Orient Express.

After You Read

1. The main purpose of page 4 is to explain:
   A. what the Orient Express represents.
   B. the route of the Orient Express.
   C. why the Orient Express departs from Paris.
   D. what kind of people ride the Orient Express.

2. Which of the following summarises what Eli says on page 7?
   A. The train ride lets passengers experience another historical era.
   B. The vehicle contains a time machine.
   C. The trip merges contemporary transportation with the past.
   D. The other passengers are trying to flee their realities.

3. According to the story, what helped the Orient Express become so famous?
   A. advertising
   B. a book
   C. the airplane
   D. the Iron Curtain

4. What opinion does the university lecturer express on page 11?
   A. The trip is only for people with authentic enthusiasm for travel.
   B. The route covers many areas of great historical significance.
   C. Writer and teachers will gain the most insight from the journey.
   D. Knowing about history will enhance the experience of riding the train.

5. The word 'winds' in the first paragraph on page 12 is closest in meaning to:
   A. rushes
   B. twists
   C. indexes
   D. collapses

6. The cabin steward refers to the Orient Express as _____ luxurious hotel on wheels.
   A. a
   B. the
   C. one
   D. some

7. Which of the following does the writer imply on page 15?
   A. The view in Austria is the most scenic of the ride.
   B. Passengers can request to eat their meals in private.
   C. The staff on the Orient Express are actual magicians.
   D. The waiters are reluctant to prepare breakfast.

8. Working on the Orient Express requires different planning skills than working in a hotel.
   A. True
   B. False
   C. Doesn't say

9. When the barman says 'it's not easy' on page 19, he is referring to:
   A. the train
   B. being a barman
   C. planning in advance
   D. running out of food and drink

10. Which of these questions cannot be answered with the information on page 20?
   A. What's one challenge faced by the employees on the train?
   B. What kinds of meals does the chef usually prepare?
   C. How does the movement of the train help servers?
   D. What is the Orient Express's usual route?

11. Which word can 'meet' be replaced with in the first paragraph on page 22?
   A. attain
   B. erode
   C. pose
   D. levy

12. Which of the following does the writer conclude on page 26?
   A. It's tough getting a ticket on the Orient Express.
   B. Most workers on the Orient Express fantasise about being passengers.
   C. Those who get to experience the Orient Express feel privileged.
   D. Passengers on the Orient Express are jealous of the staff.

Travel Temptations

The Orient Express, with its magnificent decor, fine cuisine, and careful attention to details, has long been famous for pampering its guests. Treatment like this was once available only to the rich and famous. Today, however, large hotels, or 'resorts', worldwide are offering an ever-growing range of luxurious options.

SEA RANCH LODGE, CALIFORNIA

Sea Ranch Lodge is located on the California coast, a two-hour drive north of San Francisco. Its magnificent view of the Pacific Ocean provides an ideal place to relax and enjoy nature. Fine food and wine are two of Sea Ranch Lodge's biggest attractions. The chef is famous in the region and the assistant chef is an experienced specialist baker. In addition, the lodge regularly invites local winemakers to host dinners at the resort where food and wine are perfectly paired and guests can learn more about fine dining. Because it is located far from any large city, Sea Ranch Lodge also offers an unusual option – a dark sky. Guests are encouraged to stay up late to enjoy the beauty of the stars, which are not often visible in the city.

KARMA SAMUI, THAILAND

On the tiny island of Koh Samui off the coast of Thailand lies a resort that provides an astonishing level of luxury. Guests stay in individual houses, or villas, spaced out along the beach. Each one is equipped with a kitchen, dining room, and lounge area, as well as its own medium-sized swimming

Luxury Holidays: Amenities and Facilities			
Destination	**Speciality**	**Dining Facilities**	**Activities**
Sea Ranch Lodge	magnificent views	fine cuisine paired with fine wine	• learn about wine • enjoy the stars
Karma Samui	extreme luxury	sea-view dining room or in-room private chef	• learn to cook street food
Canyon Ranch	an introduction to holistic health	healthy food with weight loss guidance	• fitness classes • hiking and biking • cooking lessons

pool. Meals are available in the dining room, or for the height of luxury, guests can have a private chef and waiter prepare and serve their meals in their villa. Karma Samui also offers a 'street food' cooking class in which guests take a guided tour of local markets, buy provisions, and then practise cooking these new specialities when they return to the resort.

CANYON RANCH, ARIZONA

Canyon Ranch calls itself a holistic, or complete, health resort. The owner, Mel Zukeman, says, 'For me, our heartfelt intention to help every guest find greater joy in living is what makes us different from all other resorts.' The aim is to teach guests how to care for and heal both their bodies and their minds. There are meetings with doctors and alternative healers who offer both conventional and unconventional treatment options. A stay also includes physical activities such as swimming and hiking, dietary guidance, as well as advice on how to reduce stress, and better manage personal issues and human interactions in everyday life. Not bad for a week's holiday!

Word Count: 408
Time: _____

Words to Know

This story is set in the country of Japan. It takes place in the northern part, in the city of Shirone.

A **The Big Kite Festival.** Read the definitions. Then complete the paragraph with the correct forms of the words.

battle: a fight between two forces or groups
enthusiastic: having an energetic interest in something
festival: a public holiday or celebration
kite: a light wooden framework covered with paper and flown
maniac: a person who acts crazy; a madman

This story is about a five-day **(1)**_____ in the northern part of Japan. During the celebration, teams of people fly **(2)**_____ over a river. The competition also involves **(3)**_____ between teams in which they try to force each other's kites out of the air. The teams become so **(4)**_____ about kites that some people call them 'Kite Crazy'. Others consider them to be **(5)**_____ who can't control themselves during the event!

B Tug of War. Read the paragraph. Then complete the definitions with the correct words or phrases.

At the Shirone kite festival, a tug of war starts after one team has pulled another team's kite out of the air. During this part of the competition, the two rivals pull on ropes to determine which team is stronger. Each team clings to their kite ropes and pulls as hard as possible. Their goal is to capture the other team's kite by breaking the ropes that hold it. These clashes are a thrilling part of the contest and everyone fights fiercely until the end.

1. A c_____ is similar to a heated argument or fight.
2. Another word for 'enemy' is r_____.
3. To c_____ is to hold on tightly to something.
4. To c_____ is to take something by force.
5. A competition which involves pulling ropes in opposite directions is a t_____ o_____ w_____.

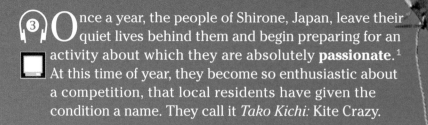

Once a year, the people of Shirone, Japan, leave their quiet lives behind them and begin preparing for an activity about which they are absolutely **passionate**.[1] At this time of year, they become so enthusiastic about a competition, that local residents have given the condition a name. They call it *Tako Kichi:* Kite Crazy.

Kazuo Tamura, a local resident and kite-flying fan, explains what 'Kite Crazy' means. 'Kite Crazy refers to people who really love kites,' he says. 'People who think more about kites than getting their three meals a day. Even when they go to bed, they can't fall asleep because they see kites flying over their beds.' Sleeplessness? Kites flying over beds? What is it about kite flying that makes the residents of Shirone so crazy?

---

[1] **passionate:** feeling very strongly about sth

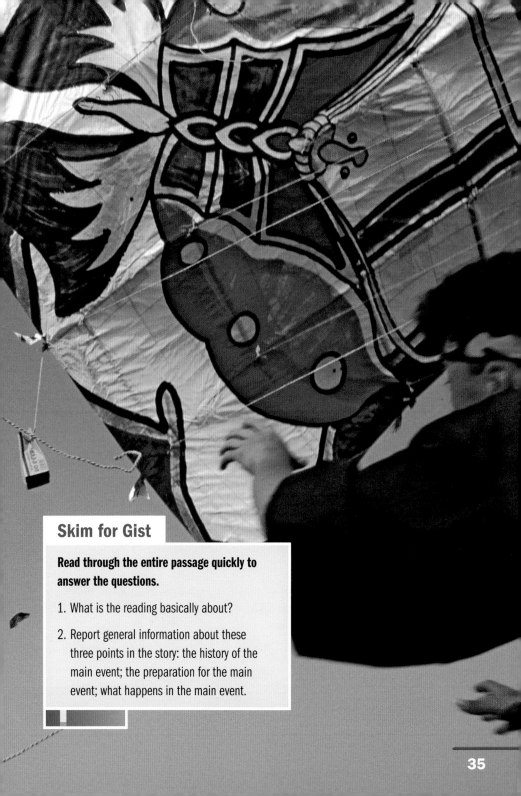

Skim for Gist

Read through the entire passage quickly to answer the questions.

1. What is the reading basically about?

2. Report general information about these three points in the story: the history of the main event; the preparation for the main event; what happens in the main event.

Normally Shirone is a quiet and peaceful place, like many other towns that are found in northern Japan. Farmers work hard through the spring to plant their rice on time, but when the work is done, they turn their attention away from the earth. They emerge from their labours ready to have some fun and join in a five-day festival that celebrates the open sky – the Great Shirone Kite Fight.

The Great Kite Fight is not a new event, but part of an old tradition that began 250 years ago. Several older paintings are still in existence which feature past great kite battles as their subject matter. These historic pieces serve to illustrate the beginnings of the festival. The kite fighting tradition actually originated from an ancient legend. According to the story, a giant kite was given to a village leader by the local **lord**.[1] The kite was so huge that it damaged houses and crops in the fields when it unexpectedly came crashing down. Soon after, villagers who were angry or upset with each other started using kites to **resolve**[2] their disagreements. The one who won the kite battle also won the argument. Eventually, these battles **evolved into**[3] a festival where people could have their battles in the sky and rid themselves of a bit of stress every spring. For a growing number of passionate kite flyers, this annual kite fight became a **prime**[4] opportunity for some 'high-level' enjoyment.

---

[1]**lord:** a man of high social status
[2]**resolve:** to find a way of dealing with disagreements
[3]**evolve into:** to gradually change and develop over a period of time
[4]**prime:** most suitable

These days, the kite festival is as popular as it ever was. Now, as with previous years, kite madness comes to Shirone every June, and it affects people of all ages. Residents both old and young join the fun and just about anybody who can cling to a piece of kite rope gets involved. The town itself is transformed into the equivalent of a giant kite factory as rival teams prepare for battle. Playgrounds, car parks, the driveways of houses, and even schools become work areas for the teams. The kite makers occupy almost every inch of free space available in order to make their huge and fantastic creations.

Kazuo Tamura is an internationally known kite-flying team leader. He feels that the kite festival is not only significant for him but also for the entire town and society as well. He explains in his own words: 'This event is very important to me. It's not just a question of having a good time. Somehow, underneath a sky that's full of kites, everyone seems equal.' Tamura's beliefs about the benefits of the Kite Fight don't stop there. He also feels that there's a peaceful element to the event as well. 'No one flies a kite in times of war. So the festival is like a sign that we're at peace.'

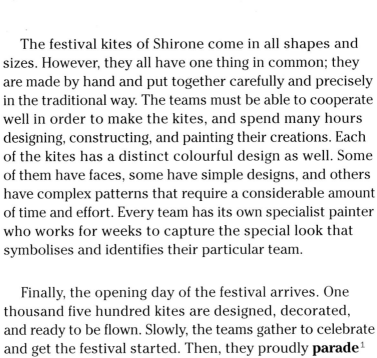

The festival kites of Shirone come in all shapes and sizes. However, they all have one thing in common; they are made by hand and put together carefully and precisely in the traditional way. The teams must be able to cooperate well in order to make the kites, and spend many hours designing, constructing, and painting their creations. Each of the kites has a distinct colourful design as well. Some of them have faces, some have simple designs, and others have complex patterns that require a considerable amount of time and effort. Every team has its own specialist painter who works for weeks to capture the special look that symbolises and identifies their particular team.

Finally, the opening day of the festival arrives. One thousand five hundred kites are designed, decorated, and ready to be flown. Slowly, the teams gather to celebrate and get the festival started. Then, they proudly **parade**[1] their newly made kites through the streets of the town on their way to the battleground of the Great Kite Fight. As marching bands play and people shout excitedly, the town gets its first look at this year's creations. The biggest kites are called *odako*. They are difficult and uncomfortable to carry and are not easy to get into the air, but 13 different teams have come to try their best to fly them. Other teams prefer the smaller kites called *rokako*, which are much easier to move through the air. One could consider them to be more like **fighter jets**[2] whereas the *odako* are more like **heavy bombers**.[3] If it all sounds a little bit like war, that's because it is; the members of these teams are here to battle, **dominate**,[4] and win!

---

[1]**parade *(verb)*:** to display proudly
[2]**fighter jet:** a small, fast plane that fights in the air
[3]**heavy bomber:** a large plane that drops bombs and other weapons
[4]**dominate:** to control

For centuries, the battle of the kites has taken place along Shirone's central river, the Nakanokuchi. The competing teams, dressed in traditional clothing, stand on opposite sides of the river as they plan and prepare to gain the best position. This long-standing tradition really is like a battle in a war. The goal is for one team to capture another team's kite by using their own kite and rope. The teams try to wrap the rope from their kite around the ropes of the rival team's kite. They then try to use their physical power to pull the rival's kite from the sky. Lots of loud shouting and cries of excitement can be heard as the teams try to capture the other teams' kites. It's an extremely **thrilling**[1] time, both for the participants and the **spectators**.[2]

Once one team has captured another team's kite, however, that's not the end of the battle; it is time for the real competition to begin. Once both kites are down, the ropes remain **twisted**[3] together and the kites can't be separated until one team drops their rope. The teams must **desperately**[4] **cling**[5] to their kite ropes, doing everything they can to keep their grip. Remember, the teams are located on the opposite sides of a river, so the first team to drop or break its rope will lose the battle and the kites will fall into the water. Therefore, these tugs of war often continue fiercely to the finish. Each team member must show strength of both mind and body as they try to pull the rival team members down so that they can no longer hang on to their kite.

---

[1]**thrilling:** extremely exciting
[2]**spectator:** sb who watches a public event
[3]**twist:** to bring together by making a circular motion
[4]**desperately:** making great effort to do sth
[5]**cling to:** to hold on to sth tightly

Unfortunately, in the tug of war between the teams, both of the kites are twisted, pulled, and basically destroyed. These kite battles often carry on for a **considerable**[1] length of time, and usually leave people wondering which team will win and which will lose. Nobody knows, but it's certainly a thrilling fight. Finally, when one team's rope breaks – usually after lots of pulling and hard work – a winner is declared. Extra points are given to the winning side for every inch of rope it captures from the losing team, and the points are recorded on a score board at the side of the river. It is obviously a competition which the locals take very seriously, but no matter who wins, there is always something lost. This become obvious as both teams' kites are left floating in the river – wet masses of paper and wood that were once the pride of the local teams.

All along the river, teams get involved in clashes that quickly lead to open war. The battles spread to the town, and almost everyone gets involved. Teams of children fight bravely against each other as the power of the wind nearly pulls them off their feet. At one point, the fighting gets so involved that the police must step in. No, not to break up a fight, but to help a group of kite fighters to cross the railway tracks! The policeman holds the team back with a stop gesture, and then finally, when the train has passed and the crossing is safe, the battle continues. The team races down the street, desperately fighting to capture the rival kite. The whole town seems to have gone mad; kite craziness is more than just an illness during the Great Kite Fight – it becomes an **epidemic!**[2]

---

[1] **considerable:** large in size, amount, or degree
[2] **epidemic:** a disease that spreads very quickly among many people

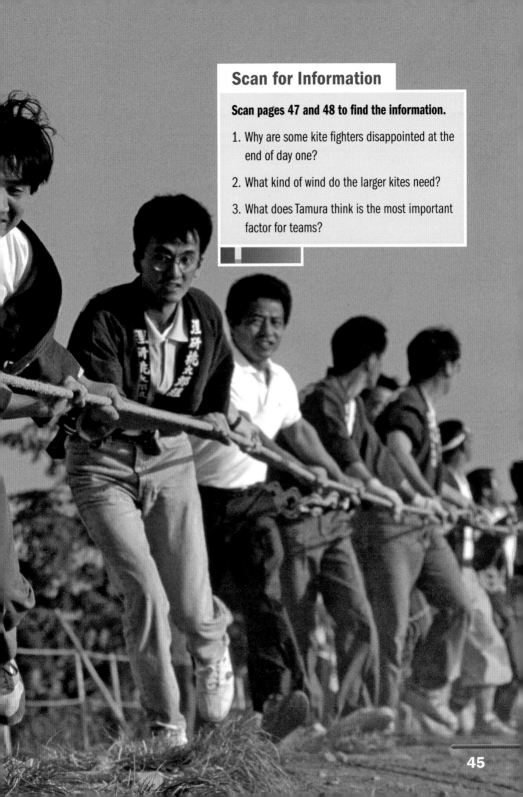

Scan for Information

Scan pages 47 and 48 to find the information.

1. Why are some kite fighters disappointed at the end of day one?

2. What kind of wind do the larger kites need?

3. What does Tamura think is the most important factor for teams?

By the end of day one, thousands of the smaller kites have been destroyed, but not everyone has been able to enjoy the competition. The large *odako* kites are still not flying. Unfortunately, the teams cannot even get the huge *odakos* into the air. The wind has been blowing from the east, and without a stable northern wind, the larger kites are helpless. They're simply too big for the wind to lift into the air. When one team tries to get theirs off the ground, it rises for a short period of time, and then falls slowly to the earth, catching itself on a building on the way down and tearing as it falls.

The *odako* teams must wait for a change in the weather, and hope that they are ready when the north wind finally arrives. While they are waiting, the teams step back from the excitement of the riverside to work on their ropes, ensuring that they are strung, or put together, correctly. The ropes used in the Shirone kite fights are made by hand, which makes them extremely strong. Very tough ropes are essential to Shirone kites because they have two purposes: first, they control the kite, and secondly they have to be able to **stand up to**[1] the fierce and **aggressive**[2] tugs of war.

---

[1] **stand up to (sth):** to resist or survive sth
[2] **aggressive:** determined; forcefully done

Each team keeps their own method of making their ropes strong a strict secret. This secrecy is part of the competitiveness and teamwork that **constitutes**[1] an important part of the kite festival. In fact, many believe that without teamwork, there might be no festival at all.

Kazuo Tamura explains what competing in the kite festival is like, stating that working together is of the greatest importance. 'The most important thing is teamwork,' he says. 'Everyone runs around clinging to the same rope, so they have to work together. This is very important. Without teamwork, these kites won't fly; they'll fall right to the ground.'

---

[1] **constitute:** refers to parts that combine to form sth

Tamura's plan for teamwork is a good one, but even the best teamwork doesn't matter if there is no wind to fly the kites. A second *odako* kite tries to make it up in the air only to fail. As it falls to the side of the river, it catches on the side of the bridge and is damaged. By the third day of this five-day festival, there is still no northern wind, and everyone is very disappointed. They all wish that the wind would pick up, but it doesn't help.

The *odako* teams are worried that this may be the first year in Shirone's history that they will not have a chance to fight; but they aren't giving up on the fun. When evening falls, the *odako* teams still manage to have a good time and celebrate the festival. They spend the evening dancing in the darkness, singing, and playing instruments. Everyone welcomes the break from the stress of the kite competition; moreover, they welcome an opportunity to relax and have a little fun. After all, that is what the five-day festival is all about for most people, giving themselves a chance to go a little crazy.

On the fifth and final day of the competition, the wind continues to deliver disappointment, but at the last minute something wonderful happens. With just one hour remaining in the event, a northern wind comes down along the river. At last, the oversized kites are released from their earthly imprisonment and lifted up into the sky. The crowds shout with happiness as the beautiful, giant *odako* kites rise high into the air at last. Now, finally, Kazuo Tamura's team will have its only chance to win a tug of war before the festival ends. It's a situation that requires both skill and passion; luckily Tamura's team has plenty of both. Tamura shouts loudly as he races down the side of the river to get his team ready. The entire group must be both excited and motivated to win.

At last, the two rival kites are lifted up into the air by the soft wind and they begin dancing slowly across the sky. As they do, the rope from one of the kites begins to wrap itself around the rope of the other. Suddenly, the two kites are wound together and go crashing towards the river. The young men on Tamura's team have managed to capture the competing team's kite and Tamura goes wild with excitement. Acting as both teacher and coach, he yells and encourages the team to work harder as the next part of the competition begins. Several metres of twisted rope lie across the river, connecting the two teams in a fierce tug of war. For the teams, the battle seems more like a matter of life and death – not just a kite competition!

The clash between the two opposing teams of kite fighters continues for quite some time. Both teams seem confident of a victory, but the results are still unsure and the battle is in full force. After a while, the teams switch techniques and start shaking the ropes up and down, hoping that maybe the weight of the kites will cause their rival's rope to break. All the while that the teams are battling, Tamura runs around his team, shouting like a madman, and cheering nonstop. One can easily see why people could say that he has gone completely Kite Crazy, but Tamura doesn't think he's all that crazy. He simply considers himself to be a big fan of the sport. 'People call me a kite **maniac**,'[1] Tamura says, laughing. 'I am a kite enthusiast. That's just me,' he argues. 'They call me a kite maniac, but I don't think I'm all that crazy.'

The two teams are nearly exhausted, but the battle continues. Neither one will stop until the war is won, but the ropes remain firmly tied together across the width of the river. Then suddenly, there's a loud sound and both teams fall backwards as the **tension**[2] of the ropes is released. One set of kite ropes has finally broken and it belongs to the opposite team. It looks like Tamura's team is the winner of the *odako* battle for this year's festival!

---

[1]**maniac:** sb who behaves in a stupid and dangerous way
[2]**tension:** the degree of tightness found when sth is stretched between points

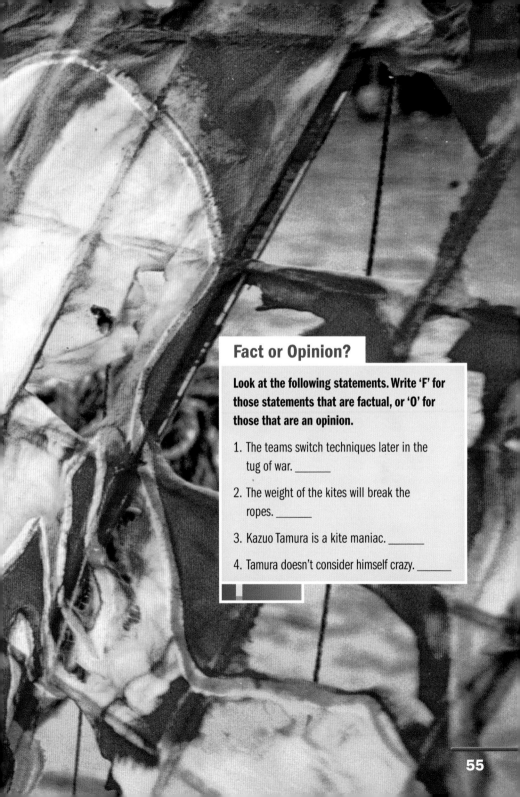

Fact or Opinion?

Look at the following statements. Write 'F' for those statements that are factual, or 'O' for those that are an opinion.

1. The teams switch techniques later in the tug of war. _____

2. The weight of the kites will break the ropes. _____

3. Kazuo Tamura is a kite maniac. _____

4. Tamura doesn't consider himself crazy. _____

So are the people of Shirone really Kite Crazy? Tamura certainly looked a little crazy when he finally had the opportunity to get into battle. But then, most of the **residents**[1] of this village certainly seem to become very excited and passionate at this time of year. If it is some type of craziness, it is definitely not a dangerous one.

As the Great Kite Fight ends for another year, the competitors – both winners and losers – begin to clean up the damaged kites. In a good year every kite is destroyed, but the people of Shirone never seem to feel sorry that they are gone. They know that next year, the kites will live again, flying across the sky until 'Kite Craziness' is no more. For now, it appears that this unusual and interesting tradition is going strong, and there are no signs that the 'Kite Crazy' epidemic will disappear any time soon. In fact, among everyone who appears affected by it, no one seems to want to find a cure.

---

[1] **resident:** sb who lives in a particular place

After You Read

1. Which word on page 34 means 'the state someone is in'?
   A. activity
   B. condition
   C. enthusiast
   D. sleeplessness

2. According to Kazuo Tamura, which of the following describes 'kite crazy'?
   A. stealing a neighbour's kite
   B. caring about kites more than food
   C. quitting a job to join the festival
   D. painting pictures of kites on the ceiling

3. What is the writer's main purpose on page 37?
   A. to introduce specific people
   B. to explain the rules of the festival
   C. to give background information
   D. to show how kites can be dangerous

4. In the second paragraph on page 41, 'them' in 'fly them' refers to:
   A. bombers
   B. jets
   C. *rokako*
   D. *odako*

5. What happens when a kite is captured?
   A. One team loses.
   B. The tug of war begins.
   C. The rope is cut.
   D. The competition is abandoned.

6. Extra points are awarded based on the:
   A. length of the rope.
   B. thrill of the fight.
   C. time spent pulling.
   D. size of the kite.

7. According to Tamura, a good wind is necessary for success in a kite battle:
    A. True
    B. False

8. Why do the people of Shirone need a chance to go a little crazy?
    A. because there is no northern wind
    B. because the kite festival is completed
    C. because they usually work very hard
    D. because they are disappointed

9. A captured kite drops _____ the river.
    A. into
    B. down
    C. from
    D. on

10. What does the writer probably think about the *odako* battle on page 53?
    A. It's upsetting to watch.
    B. They are using minimum effort.
    C. It will have a tragic ending.
    D. It's a little too serious.

11. A suitable heading for page 54 is:
    A. Team Cuts Rope With Knife
    B. Madman Rushes Into Festival
    C. Thrilling Championship Battle
    D. Yelling Wakes Neighbours

12. What conclusion does the writer make in the last paragraph?
    A. Kite flying should become the national sport of Japan.
    B. The people of Shirone are proud of their kite tradition.
    C. No one can understand why the festival is popular.
    D. After the festival, competitors should go to hospital.

Competing with Kites Around the World

KITE FIGHTS

Historians believe that people first started to fly kites thousands of years ago either in India, Afghanistan, or any other Asian country, depending upon the source. Somewhere in the early history of kite flying, the idea of having battles in the sky was born. One area well known for its fighter kites is India. There, kites called 'patang' or 'guda' are flown, and the rope used to fly them is coated with broken bits of glass. The winner is the one who is able to cut the ropes of all of the other competitors. Afghan fighter kites are much larger than their Indian cousins with some being up to five feet wide. They are usually constructed of different materials, and competitors use very lightweight paper for their creations.

The sport of kite fighting is also popular in such places as Japan, Korea, Thailand, parts of Europe, Cuba, and Brazil. Brazilian kites are often smaller constructions, but the competition between rivals is still just as enthusiastic. Part of the fun of kite fighting in Brazil involves cutting away someone else's kite and then stealing it. Trees and power lines in Brazilian cities are often full of lost or abandoned kites.

Score Chart for the 2008 Kitemaker's Competition

Entry Name	Flight 3	Bopper	Go Boy	Higher
Maker's Name	B. Okano	J. Diaz	L. Shen	S. Smith
Appearance Score out of 10	8.27	7.57	7.50	7.70
Flight Score out of 10	7.57	7.43	7.83	7.10
Construction Score out of 10	8.57	8.27	8.27	8.44
Design Score out of 10	7.82	8.23	7.50	7.33
Total Score out of 40	32.33	31.50	31.10	30.57

KITE-BUILDING COMPETITIONS

Kite-building competitions offer a totally different approach to the sport of kite flying. Each year, hundreds of festivals are held around the world in which people build their own kites and bring them to be judged by experts in the field. The American Kitefliers Association was formed over 40 years ago and today it is the largest such organisation in the world with over 4,000 members in 35 countries. During the annual competitions, kites are judged on four characteristics: appearance, flight capability, construction technique, and design.

The kite's 'appearance' is simply a measure of how good the kite looks on the ground. The 'flight capability' category measures how well the flier is able to handle it. 'Construction technique' refers to how neatly and carefully the kite was made, and the 'design' category is a measure of how strong the structure of the kite is. Judges carefully assess all attributes when making their decisions. Although it's a fun sport, competitors take it very seriously and work extremely hard on their entries. You can research possible kite-building competitions in your area by going to the Kitefliers Association website.

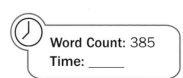

Word Count: 385
Time: _____

Words to Know

This story is set in the town of Greve, which is in the region of Tuscany, Italy.

 A Quiet Little Town. Read the paragraph. Then complete the definitions with the correct <u>underlined</u> word.

Greve is a <u>quaint</u> little town in northern Italy. Near the centre of the large wine-producing area of Chianti, the village is surrounded by <u>vineyards</u> and is also famous for its delicious *pecorino* cheese. Despite its size, Greve has become well known in recent years, largely because its <u>mayor</u> was one of the founders of the 'Slow City' movement. The principle of the movement is to fight the negative effects of <u>globalisation</u> by creating an atmosphere that allows people to slow down, relax, and enjoy.

1. the elected head of a town or city's government: _____

2. areas with plants that produce wine grapes: _____

3. when things all over the world become more similar: _____

4. attractive because it is unusual and old-fashioned: _____

5. a type of hard Italian cheese made from sheep's milk: _____

vineyards

B **The 'Slow City' Movement.** Read the paragraph. Then match each word or phrase with the correct definition.

To qualify as an official member of the Slow City movement, a town must meet Slow City standards for avoiding life in the fast lane. There is a Slow City manifesto that contains 55 criteria grouped into six general categories, including things like 'Hospitality and Community' and 'Slow City Awareness'. Towns wishing to become Slow Cities are vetted and assessed according to these criteria. In addition, they must offer their own special character, something unique to prevent the world from becoming bland and boring.

1. life in the fast lane _____

2. manifesto _____

3. hospitality _____

4. vet *(verb)* _____

5. bland _____

a. a policy document

b. examine something carefully

c. an expression referring to a fast-paced, high-pressure lifestyle

d. lacking in taste or interest

e. friendly and generous behaviour towards others, especially by giving food, drink, and a comfortable place to be

The Town of Greve in the Chianti Area

pecorino **cheese**

The fertile hills between the ancient cities of Florence and Siena in the northern Italian region of Tuscany are exceptionally beautiful. Dotted with old-fashioned houses and old farms, this rolling landscape attracts visitors from around the world and is also the home of some of the world's best-known vineyards. This area, known as Chianti, is one of Italy's most famous wine regions and a region that has grown wine grapes for centuries.

The richly-coloured dark grapes that hang on the **vines**[1] that cover these hills are lovingly cared for by the local wine growers. They carefully tend to their vineyards as a way to ensure a good harvest and as part of the well-established wine-growing tradition in the region. Once ready, the grapes are pressed to make one of Italy's most well-known red wines, Chianti. It's a wine that is exported all over the world and enjoyed in homes and restaurants from Rome to New York. Near the centre of this wine-producing area, one can find the **quaint**[2] little town of Greve.

---

[1]**vine:** a plant that grows up and over things, some of which produce grapes
[2]**quaint:** interesting with a slightly strange and old-fashioned quality

Greve or 'Greve in Chianti' to give its full name, is a quiet, modest town that has a population of only a few thousand people. Despite its size, it is the regional centre for wine trade, as well as a centre for the trade of local products. The food market of the town shows the full richness of the local harvest, offering fruit and vegetables from the surrounding countryside in addition to delicious cheeses, olive oil, sausages, and ham. It is truly a place where the quality of life has become evident in the richness of its products.

The town's quaintness, its hospitality, and the **lushness**[1] and diversity of the **undulating**[2] landscape that surrounds it have long attracted tourists and travellers to the region. The current flow of tourism to the area is most often directly related to the **viniculture**[3] and the various enterprises associated with it, which help to form a highly integrated and productive local economy. It's a busy little town, but while it is full of activity, it is also a village that appreciates tradition – and a place where time is rarely rushed.

---

[1] **lushness:** fertility
[2] **undulating:** rolling; to move or shaped like waves that are rising and falling
[3] **viniculture:** the growing of grapes for wine

Even on market day, as people walk through the streets, stopping in one place to try the cheese or stopping in another to examine the produce, the mood of the town is distinctively relaxed. Greve is a place where time never seems to be hurried and life often seems more leisurely. Greve's residents sincerely make an effort to spend time with their families and friends, to take pleasure in life, and to really live their lives to the fullest.

Throughout the day, groups of people **stroll**[1] down the streets of the beautiful town, shopping, tasting the produce, enjoying the atmosphere, and conversing with nearly everyone as they go. The town's culture is **inherently**[2] slow, which makes Greve more than simply slow paced; it makes it, in fact, an official Slow City and one that is quite proud of this special status. Greve is not an exception, a single slow-moving city attempting to save traditional culture; it is part of an organised movement. There are now several of these unusual cities throughout the country of Italy as well as in a number of other countries, too.

---

[1]**stroll:** to walk in a leisurely way; walk slowly
[2]**inherently:** a necessary and natural quality of sth

69

Paolo Saturnini is the mayor of Greve and one of the founders of the phenomenon known as 'Slow Cities'. Together with the mayors from three other small Italian towns, Saturnini created the Slow Cities group, which is referred to as *Cittaslow* in Italian, in 1999. Subsequently, several other cities with fewer than 50,000 residents joined the group, making it first a national movement and later an international one.

The mission of the Slow City movement is to keep the hometowns of its members free from a life in the fast lane. To help accomplish this mission, the group aims to improve the quality of life in smaller towns and villages while resisting the fast-paced, globalised atmosphere that is so often seen in big cities throughout the world. Nowadays, many villages and towns worldwide are applying to join the Slow City movement, but not every town is qualified.

Cities that are interested in joining the movement are first **vetted**[1] to see if they meet the organisation's criteria. Once accepted, they must agree to follow a strict set of detailed clauses within the Slow Cities **manifesto**[2] to ensure the movement's standards are maintained. The basic idea behind these criteria is to encourage cities to **cherish**[3] what makes their community unique and different. One of the manifesto's criteria is the promotion of local produce and products; another is the encouragement of maintaining cultural identity within the city. Saturnini explains: 'Our challenge and our duty is to try to maintain the soul, the essence, the "specialness" of Greve in Chianti, and all the other Slow Cities.'

---

[1]**vet:** to check sth carefully to make sure it is suitable
[2]**manifesto:** a formal statement expressing the aims of an organisation
[3]**cherish:** to treasure; take care of

Sequence the Events

**What is the correct order of the events?
Write numbers.**

_____ Other Italian cities joined the
Slow Cities group.

_____ Cities from outside Italy joined
the Slow Cities.

_____ The mayor of Greve and two other
mayors founded the Slow Cities league.

_____ Many towns and cities worldwide
applied to join the Slow Cities
movement.

Alongside the Slow City movement, another subsidiary movement has developed: the Slow Food movement. This secondary movement is similar to the Slow City movement and some of the supporting concepts of the two groups overlap. The main difference is that the Slow Food movement differs in focus. Its **practitioners**[1] aim to preserve the pleasures of good, locally grown, high-quality food. The concept of Slow Food contrasts the tendency for people to eat unhealthy 'fast foods' without restraint, a tendency that seems to have taken hold around the world. Those who follow the Slow Food movement prefer not to turn to easy, low-quality methods of food preparation, and continue to use classic, traditional methods of food preparation.

With the tremendous success of the Slow Food movement in Italy, the movement has now gone international and has more than 80,000 members in over 100 countries worldwide. The enthusiastic response to the notion may be an indication that people around the globe are concerned with the increased popularity of fast food.

This means that in Greve, a quick hamburger for the evening meal isn't the easy answer, but that's no problem here. Sandro Checcuci, a resident of Greve, explains that living in a place that values slow food makes it easy to do everything slowly. 'It's very nice to live here,' he says, 'because we have a nice atmosphere, we have nice landscapes and so, when you have nice things to see, [and] a nice place to live in, it's very easy.'

---

[8]**practitioner:** sb who does a particular activity

The Slow Food movement is not limited to the kitchen, either. It also encourages the **intrinsic**[1] value of taking time to enjoy dining. Around the town of Greve, people everywhere can be seen relaxing and dining together, slowly drinking wine and enjoying their meal. In this region, it's not about efficiency or the rush to get to the television, it's about enjoying time with family and friends and taking a moment to truly taste how delicious the food is.

While the foods of Greve are wonderfully delicious, such taste does take time and effort to create. To prepare slow food, chefs must appreciate the importance of cooking in a more traditional way and focusing on taste and health. Chef Salvatore Toscano is one of those chefs. He used to manage an American-style restaurant in Florence, where he spent his days preparing and serving hamburgers – a symbol of fast food around the world. Then five years ago, he left all that behind and moved to Greve, where he opened a new, different type of restaurant. He now cooks slow food, using fresh local produce and the results are delicious. Toscano explains what 'living slow' means to him: 'It means taking the time, finding the rhythm that lets you live more calmly in a lot of ways, starting, of course, with what you eat.' Salvatore even finds the time to come out of his restaurant kitchen and talk to his customers to ask them how they enjoyed the food. Such behaviour is often rare in the fast-paced modern world and it serves as a reminder that dining 'slow' can be an enjoyable experience for everyone involved.

---

[1] **intrinsic:** relating to the essential features of sth or sb

Another local example of slow food can be found in the mountains of Pistoia in northern Tuscany. Here, generations of farmers have produced a famous *pecorino* cheese that is said to be delightfully unique. Made from the raw milk of black sheep, the cheese is **hand moulded**[1] twice a day. The process is long and labour-intensive as each cheese is individually pressed and shaped – but the result of all that labour and care can be uniformly delicious. There is often nothing quite like food that has been prepared by hand rather than mass produced.

The tradition of making hand-moulded *pecorino* had been dying out until the Slow Food movement stepped in. The group developed a special promotion to organise the farmers and promote the cheese itself. These days, cheese production is on the increase again and cheese makers like Luana Pagliai have been able to continue making and selling their own *pecorino*. On the farm, they work quickly and carefully to gather the sheep's milk using a time-tested technique. After milking the sheep, the cheese-making process begins. They first mix the milk with a few special ingredients to make the basic form of cheese. After that, it is moulded and packed twice daily until it becomes the magnificent delicacy that has made the region famous. Pagliai explains how the Slow Food movement has really helped her and her product. 'It's brought us a kind of fame,' she says. 'Not everyone knew about our product. The project is getting us noticed.'

---

[1] **hand mould:** to mould into a shape using one's hands

Slow-Food farmer Luciano Bertini sums up the importance of the Slow Food movement in today's fast-paced, **homogenised**[1] world. According to him, it's about making sure that everything in the world doesn't become exactly the same and that the world doesn't become **bland**[2] and boring. 'From Singapore to Macau,' he says, 'in New York and Rome, you always find the same pizza, the same hamburgers. Slow Food doesn't want this. Slow Food wants the specialness of every product to be respected.' For Bertini, the Slow Food movement is about the quality of life and maintaining the **integrity**[3] of the local products and atmosphere, rather than rushing to become part of one global movement or another.

Bertini, Saturnini, and all of the other residents of Greve in Chianti and other Slow Cities may just **be on to**[4] something. They are making a unified effort to maintain a high quality of life and to prevent the world from becoming bland. While it may seem to be an unusual approach for some, their liberal way of thinking may just be what the world needs. After all, in years to come, they may be able to look back with great satisfaction. They will have been enjoying life while most of the rest of the world has been rushing through it. They will have enjoyed themselves and taken it easy in the slow lane.

---

[1]**homogenise:** to make to look exactly the same as everything else
[2]**bland:** not interesting or original
[3]**integrity:** the quality of being in a good condition
[4]**be on to (sth):** to discover sth important or profitable

Infer Meaning

1. What does Bertini mean by 'the specialness of every product'? Give examples from the story.

2. What is meant by 'take it easy in the slow lane'? Write a definition.

After You Read

1. Which word on page 64 can be replaced by 'extraordinarily'?
   A. exceptionally
   B. best-known
   C. richly
   D. carefully

2. According to the information on page 67, which of the following is true about Greve?
   A. The population is exactly 6,000 people.
   B. It's a regional centre for the trade of local specialties.
   C. The fruit market attracts many tourists.
   D. It is a place where time is constantly rushed.

3. Which of the following summarises the last two lines on page 67?
   A. The town is busy, so therefore people don't celebrate tradition.
   B. The town's tradition is to stay busy with activity.
   C. While the town is active, its people don't hurry through their days.
   D. Since the people of the town don't rush time, they are not very active.

4. What are people strolling given as an example of in the second paragraph on page 68?
   A. How residents enjoy the slow pace of life in Greve.
   B. How shoppers talk to sellers in the market.
   C. How scenic and beautiful Greve is.
   D. How Greve became an official Slow City.

5. What does 'it' refer to in the first paragraph on page 70?
   A. Greve
   B. *Cittaslow*
   C. a mayor
   D. a group of cities

6. Which of the following describes a fast city?
   A. A city that cherishes what makes it original.
   B. A city that supports what is made and grown locally.
   C. A city that has developed a globalised atmosphere.
   D. A city that actively encourages maintaining a cultural identity.

7. Which of the following is an appropriate heading for page 73?
   A. Declining Food Movement
   B. Slow Food, High Quality
   C. Modern Methods Only
   D. Greve Bans Hamburgers

8. In the second paragraph on page 74, the word 'intrinsic' describes something:
   A. coherent
   B. inherent
   C. liberal
   D. rigid

9. On page 74, Salvatore Toscano is given as a example of someone who:
   A. altered his life to follow the Slow Food philosophy.
   B. believes that eating Slow Food requires sacrifice.
   C. enjoys dining in restaurants.
   D. anticipates that all people will change their eating habits.

10. Which of the following questions cannot be answered by the information on page 77?
   A. From what animal's milk is *pecorino* cheese made?
   B. What does Luana Pagliai do for a career?
   C. What special ingredients go into *pecorino* cheese?
   D. How was the tradition of making *pecorino* cheese rescued?

11. What opinion does Luciano Bertini express on page 78?
   A. Singapore and Macau lack any forms of regional food.
   B. Uniqueness is an important aspect of slow food.
   C. Quality of life is more important than the taste of food.
   D. People should be suspicious of global movements.

12. What does the writer probably think about the Slow City and Slow Food movements?
   A. Neither prevents the world from being bland.
   B. Both promote escaping modern work.
   C. Neither is a very liberal philosophy.
   D. Both are positive ways of thinking.

HEINLE Times

SLOW FOOD AND MORE

The Slow Movement is composed of a variety of groups worldwide that advocate paying careful attention to the beauty and pleasure available around us, instead of rushing through life.

Slow Food

The Slow Food movement has been growing slowly but steadily since it was started in 1986. It was developed in response to the opening of a hamburger restaurant near the Spanish Steps in Rome, Italy. Today there are several hundred regional groups in over 100 nations worldwide. In 2008, a group in San Francisco sponsored a Slow Food Nation event where 60,000 people convened. In 2004, the organisation opened the University of Gastronomic Sciences in Bra, Italy, to promote awareness of good food and nutrition.

Slow Cities

Like the Slow Food movement, the Slow Cities movement started in Italy. Its followers believe that cities should retain as much of their originality as possible to preserve their beauty and charm. This involves creating strict rules as to where cars can and can't go and what businesses are allowed to operate in the city. Pedestrians and cyclists are given priority over motor vehicles, and supermarkets and coffee shops with hundreds of identical stores are not welcome. There are currently 42 Slow Cities in Italy and many more in Germany, The United Kingdom, Spain, and elsewhere.

Slow Homes

Slow Home is a movement founded by John Brown, a professor of architecture at

Fast Facts about the Slow Food Nation Conference in San Francisco, September, 2008	
Duration of the Event	4 days
Farmers Chosen to Participate	60
People Who Tried 'Slow on the Go' Foods	24,000
Bags of Fresh Fruits and Vegetables Sold	35,000
Total People Estimated in Attendance	60,000

SOURCE: http://slowfoodnation.org

the University of Calgary in Canada. He and his group believe that most new houses are being built cheaply and easily, but are unoriginal and boring. Therefore, the Slow Home movement encourages people to avoid standardised housing. According to Professor Brown, it is important for people to learn about design and construction when building a home and to become involved with making intelligent decisions about the place where they will spend so much of their lives.

Slow Travel

In this age of superhighways and jet planes, some people are talking about slowing down the travel experience. In 2008, two Swedish tour companies offered 8,000 train trips to various destinations in Europe. Typically, if one were to take a plane, the trips would take two hours on average. Alternatively, the train journeys take a day or two. Despite the longer time needed, the programme was extremely popular and better for the environment, releasing about 20 per cent less harmful gas into the atmosphere than the same trip made by car or plane.

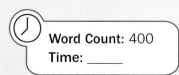

Word Count: 400
Time: _____

Grammar Focus: Metaphors

- You use a metaphor as a device to make a comparison or draw a parallel. Metaphors use words in a way that is different from how you normally use them, in order to make language more interesting.
  After a long day at work, her brain was fried.
  He's <u>fishing</u> for answers.
- Metaphors can appear as nouns, adjectives, and verbs.
  Ever since our argument, I feel there is a <u>wall</u> between us.
  I can't get this <u>stubborn</u> stain out.
  Our teacher really <u>moved</u> us when he talked about his childhood in Vietnam.
- People often confuse metaphors with similes, which make a comparison using *like* or *as*.

Grammar Practice: Metaphors

A. Write the correct verb in the correct form to complete the metaphor in each sentence.

weave	starve	pepper	~~crawl~~	grasp

e.g. The train *crawled* across the countryside.

1. David finally _____ the meaning of his father's words.

2. Kate was _____ for breakfast when she woke up.

3. That author likes to _____ the lives of her character together in interesting ways.

4. My grandfather used to always _____ his stories with funny jokes.

Grammar Practice: Metaphors

B. Choose the correct travel word to complete each metaphor.

| journey | road | place | sailed | ~~transport~~ |

e.g. My grandmother's stories always _transport_ us back in time.

1. I _____ through the easy problems on the test.

2. It's been a rocky _____ for Charlie to his graduation, but he made it.

3. Brian is one of my favourite people; he has a special _____ in my heart.

4. Their marriage has been a wonderful _____ .

Grammar Focus: Hope vs. Wish

- Use *hope* to talk about something you want to happen. The verb that follows *hope* is usually in the present tense although it refers to the future.
  I <u>hope</u> that I do well on my test.
- Use *wish* for imagined situations or to say that you'd like the present situation to be different. The verb that follows *wish* is in a past tense.
  I <u>wish</u> I played the piano.
  I <u>wish</u> that today was Saturday.
- The relative pronoun *that* is optional after wish/hope.
  I <u>wish</u> (that) it would snow.
  We <u>hope</u> (that) you can come to the party.
- Use *wish it would* to say you're sorry that something won't happen.
  I <u>wish</u> it would snow. NOT: I wish it snowed.
- We don't use hope it would except in the past tense:
  I hoped it would. NOT: I hope it would

Grammar Practice: Hope vs. Wish

Arrange each sentence in the correct order with the correct form of each verb.

e.g. hope/Tamura/win again next year/ his team
  <u>Tamura hopes his team wins again next year.</u>

1. wish/some people/happen twice a year/the festival

   _____

2. hope/the town/come for the festival/many tourists

   _____

3. wish/the children/can have ice-cream every day/ they

   _____

Grammar Focus: Future Perfect Continuous

■ You form the future perfect continuous by *will + have been + present participle*.
By the year 2070, humans <u>will have been travelling</u> in space for over 100 years.

■ You use the future perfect simple to show that an action will be finished by a specific point in the future. The future perfect continuous emphasises that the action has been ongoing over a duration of time and could continue past the specific point mentioned.
By the time she graduates, Julia <u>will have been studying</u> English for three years.

■ Sentences with the future perfect continuous often include a reference to a duration of time and often begin with a separate time clause with a verb in a present tense.

Grammar Practice: Future Perfect Continuous

Choose the correct verb to complete each sentence with the future perfect continuous.

| ~~grow~~ | live | act | run | eat |

e.g. By 2029, the Slow City movement *<u>will have been growing</u>* for 30 years.

1. By the time the dessert arrives, we _____ this meal for three hours.

2. When I become a grandparent, my family _____ in this town for seven generations.

3. Next year, she _____ in that same role on stage for ten years.

4. At the end of this week, I will _____ every morning for three months!

87

Video Practice

A. Watch the video of *The Orient Express* and write the number you hear.

1. 'These days, this luxurious train makes the journey once a year – and it's a _____-day journey some wait a lifetime to take.'
2. 'For most of the _____ passengers on this run, the pampering and luxury of this famous voyage are a once-in-a-lifetime treat.'
3. 'Therefore, the Orient Express suspended its service until _____, when the route between Paris and Istanbul was restarted.'

B. Watch the video again and circle the correct preposition.

1. 'The idea isn't really to simply arrive somewhere, it's to have an incredible experience (on/along) the way.'
2. 'The work on the train has been done by an army of well-trained staff (for/over) years.'
3. 'There are certainly challenges unique to running a five-star hotel (on/upon) wheels.'

C. Watch the video again and underline the incorrect word or phrase. Write the correct one.

1. 'Still, each trip is a learning experience, including learning to stay on your feet while serving world-class cuisine.' _____
2. 'The kitchens are completely restocked within seconds to keep the train right on track.' _____
3. 'The people who travel and work on the Orient Express have a window-seat view of the world passing before their eyes ...'

_____

Video Practice

D. Watch the video of *The Great Kite Fight* and write the word you hear.

1. '... when the work is done, they're ready to have some fun at a five-day _____ that celebrates the open sky ...'
2. 'The Great Kite Fight began 250 years ago. According to _____, a giant kite was given to a village leader by the local lord.'
3. 'The town is transformed into a giant kite factory as rival teams prepare for _____.'
4. 'Each kite has a distinct colourful design to capture the special look that symbolises a _____ team.'

E. Watch the video again and circle the word you hear.

1. 'They're difficult to get into the air, but 13 different teams have come to try their (hardest/best).'
2. 'The goal is for one team to capture another team's kite and (pull/take) it from the sky.'
3. 'The battles often spread to the town, and (nearly/almost) everyone gets involved.'
4. Without a stable northern wind, the larger kites are (useless/helpless).'

F. Watch the video again and underline the incorrect word. Write the correct one.

1. 'With just one hour remaining, a southern wind comes down along the river.' _____
2. 'Neither will stop until the war is won, but the ropes remain firmly tied together over the river.' _____
3. 'But if it's some type of craziness, it's not an interesting one.' _____

Video Practice

G. Watch the video of *Living in the Slow Lane* and underline the incorrect word. Write the correct one.

1. 'But while it's full of activity, it's also a city that appreciates tradition.' _____
2. 'The town's culture is inherently slow, which has helped to make Greve an official Slow City and part of an international Slow Movement.' _____
3. 'The manifesto of the movement is to improve the condition of life in smaller towns and villages ...' _____
4. 'Now the movement has gone international, having more than 80,000 members in over 500 countries worldwide. _____

H. Watch the video again and circle the word you hear.

1. 'He used to manage an American-style restaurant in Florence, where he spent his (time/days) serving up hamburgers.'
2. 'Here, generations of farmers have produced a magnificent *pecorino* cheese that is said to be (exceptionally/delightfully) unique.'
3. 'The tradition was dying out until the Slow Food movement stepped in with a special (campaign/promotion) to organise the farmers and promote the cheese.'
4. 'They're making an effort to maintain a high quality of (life/food), and to prevent the world from becoming bland.'

(1) As the Orient Express makes its six-day journey from Paris to Istanbul, the passengers are treated to some of the best-prepared food in Europe. (2) The elegant meals include fine wines and feature several courses. (3) Although this historic trip between Paris and Istanbul only happens once a year, it takes that long for the kitchen staff to make all the preparations. (4) Because storage space on the train is limited, they have to determine exactly how much of everything they will need. (5) If they run out during the trip, they aren't always in a position to replenish their supply. (6) The chef is in charge of planning where and when provisions will be purchased along the way and when the train does stop, the kitchen staff have to move very quickly. (7) Another challenge is working in a confined space while everything swings from side to side. (8) Chef Bodiguel says, 'For me it's very difficult because we have a small kitchen and it's moving, moving, moving.' (9) Carrying drinks in the swaying train also requires careful attention. (10) However, despite these problems it appears that the passengers are enjoying the most delicious meals available anywhere in Europe.

A. Read the paragraph and answer the questions.

1. In sentence 4 the word 'they' refers to _____.
   A. meals
   B. several courses
   C. kitchen staff
   D. preparations

2. The writer probably thinks that _____.
   A. the chef on the Orient Express has a difficult job
   B. it is impossible to prepare excellent food on a train
   C. there should be more storage space on the train
   D. the food on the Orient Express used to taste better

3. Where should this sentence go? On the days he wants to serve fresh fish, he must plan where to obtain it.
   After sentence _____.

4. The paragraph is mainly about _____.
   A. the difficulties of providing delicious meals during a train trip
   B. how to prepare fine food
   C. why the kitchen staff have to plan so carefully
   D. the supplies purchased during the journey

5. The style of the furnishing of a place refers to its _____.
   A. bygone era
   B. decor
   C. cuisine
   D. terrain

6. The water from the heavy rain _____ down the street and into the gutter.
   A. walked
   B. ate
   C. poured
   D. whispered

7. Which underlined word is incorrect?
   The country <u>has</u> been destroyed <u>by</u> war, but it is <u>finally</u> on the <u>forest</u> toward peace.
   A. has
   B. by
   C. finally
   D. forest

8. The _____ supervised the waiters as they served dinner.
   A. barman
   B. cabin steward
   C. chef
   D. maitre d'

B. Read the sentences. Write 'True' or 'False'. Refer to the paragraph if necessary.

9. The Orient Express stops to collect additional provisions from time to time. _____

10. It takes a year for the kitchen staff to plan the food for the trip. _____

EXIT TEST: THE GREAT KITE FIGHT

(1) The annual kite fighting festival in Shirone, Japan is a five-day celebration involving practically everyone in the city. **(2)** Thirteen different teams will be competing with one another and the event involves the making and flying of more than 1,500 kites. **(3)** Each team has a specialist painter and its members cooperate closely on the planning, construction, and painting of their kites. **(4)** Some of the complex designs require weeks to complete. **(5)** During the giant kite fights, competing teams stand on opposite sides of the Nakanokuchi River, dressed in traditional clothing, ready for battle. **(6)** The goal is to capture another team's kite and make it crash into the river. **(7)** The team whose kite falls into the water first loses. **(8)** The team wraps the ropes of their kite around the ropes of the other team's kite while it is still in the air. **(9)** Once one kite has captured another, the two teams begin a tug of war across the river. **(10)** When one team's ropes finally break, the winner is decided. **(11)** The winning team gets extra points for every inch of rope they are able to capture from their rivals. **(12)** By the end, all the kites are destroyed, but the kite-crazy competitors don't seem to mind at all.

A. Read the paragraph and answer the questions.

11. The Shirone kite fighting festival _____.
- **A.** is not a competition
- **B.** features tiny kites
- **C.** involves swimming in a river
- **D.** includes a tug of war

12. How many kites are featured in the festival?
- **A.** 5
- **B.** 13
- **C.** 250
- **D.** over 1,500

13. As soon as a kite is down, _____.
- **A.** the ropes holding it are broken immediately
- **B.** the length of the ropes is measured
- **C.** the tug or war begins
- **D.** the two teams go across the river

14. A fight between two forces or groups is called _____.
- **A.** a cling
- **B.** a battle
- **C.** an enthusiasm
- **D.** a capture

15. Where should this sentence go?
The broken rope is then measured.

After sentence _____

16. The two _____ both wanted to win first prize.
  A. rivals
  B. clings
  C. captures
  D. kites

17. We _____ the team good luck as they prepared for the kite fight.
  A. wish
  B. wished
  C. hope
  D. hoped

18. Which underlined word is incorrect?
I <u>wish</u> that you <u>have</u> a good time <u>when</u> you <u>visit</u> Shirone for the kite festival next year.
  A. wish
  B. have
  C. when
  D. visit

B. Read the sentences. Write 'True' or 'False'. Refer to the paragraph if necessary.

19. The word 'its' in sentence 3 refers to the team. _____

20. The tug of war is usually over very quickly. _____

(1) The Slow Food movement seeks to preserve the enjoyment of simple, locally grown high-quality food. (2) Slow food is always carefully prepared and with great attention to detail. (3) A perfect example of such a product can be found in the mountains of Tuscany in northern Italy. (4) In this region, known as Pistoia, generations of farmers have specialised in producing a very unusual type of cheese called *pecorino*, made from the milk of black sheep. (5) Making this cheese requires a great deal of time and attention. (6) Each individual cheese must be moulded by hand, which involves pressing and reshaping it twice a day every day, until it is ready to eat. (7) At one point, the production of *pecorino* cheese was beginning to decrease, but then the Slow Food movement came to the rescue. (8) They put together a special programme to organise the farmers and to advertise the cheese more widely. (9) Now the cheese makers have been able to increase their production of this magnificent delicacy which is very satisfying to them and also helps ensure that future generations will be able to enjoy this unusual 'slow cheese'.

A. Read the paragraph and answer the questions.

21. *Pecorino* cheese _____.
   A. is made from goats' milk
   B. is less popular now than in the past
   C. must be handled twice a day
   D. is produced in many different places in Italy

22. In sentence 9, the word 'them' refers to _____.
   A. the cheese makers
   B. the Slow Food people
   C. the cheese
   D. future generations

23. Which statement is probably true?
   A. *Pecorino* is easier to produce than some other cheese.
   B. The Slow Food movement operates outside of Italy.
   C. Farmers all over Italy produce *pecorino* cheese.
   D. All cheese must be handled every day.

24. To examine something carefully is to _____ it.
   A. vet
   B. bland
   C. quaint
   D. globalise

25. The _____ of our hosts immediately made us feel comfortable.
   A. mayor
   B. infrastructure
   C. manifesto
   D. hospitality

26. By the time he finishes his speech, he _____ without stopping for over two hours.
   A. will talk
   B. will have been talking
   C. will be talking
   D. will have talk

27. Which underlined word is incorrect?
   <u>By</u> the end <u>of</u> next year, Sally will <u>be</u> living with <u>her</u> uncle for over four years.
   A. By
   B. of
   C. be
   D. her

B. Read the sentences. Write 'True' or 'False'. Refer to the paragraph if necessary.

28. The Slow Food movement promotes only cheese-based products. _____

29. The production of *pecorino* cheese is up because the Slow Food programme helped promote it. _____

30. The main idea of this passage is that *pecorino* is the best cheese produced in Italy. _____

Key 答案

The Orient Express
Words to Know: A. 1. f **2.** g **3.** d **4.** c **5.** h **6.** e **7.** b **8.** a **B. 1.** maitre d'
2. barman **3.** chef **4.** cabin steward
Skim for Gist: 1. A historical train that travels across Europe once a year.
The journey is meaningful and memorable for all aboard. **2.** guests and
staff
Identify Cause and Effect: 1. The development of airline travel after 1945
meant that luxury train travel was no longer as popular. **2.** Some people
are attracted to travelling on the Orient Express after reading a famous
story about it. **3.** The idea of experiencing the past motivates many
people to take a journey on the Orient Express.
Infer meaning: (suggested answers) **1.** where the guests can't see what's
happening **2.** keep the daily operations going smoothly
After You Read: 1. A **2.** A **3.** B **4.** B **5.** B **6.** A **7.** B **8.** A **9.** C **10.** B **11.** A **12.** C

The Great Kite Fight
Words to Know: A. 1. festival **2.** kites **3.** battles **4.** enthusiastic
5. maniacs **B. 1.** clash **2.** rival **3.** cling **4.** capture **5.** tug of war
Skim for Gist: (suggested answers) **1.** A town's passion over a yearly kite
festival **2.** It's been going on for hundreds of years; they build their kites
by hand; teams with giant kites compete against each other.
Scan for Information: 1. The *odako* kites aren't in the air yet. **2.** a stable
northern wind **3.** working together, teamwork
Fact or Opinion?: 1. F **2.** F **3.** O **4.** F
After You Read: 1. B **2.** B **3.** C **4.** D **5.** B **6.** A **7.** B **8.** C **9.** A **10.** D **11.** C **12.** B

Living in the Slow Lane
Words to Know: A. 1. mayor **2.** vineyards **3.** globalisation **4.** quaint
5. *pecorino* **B. 1.** c **2.** a **3.** e **4.** b **5.** d
Sequence the Events: 2, 3, 1, 4
Infer Meaning: (suggested answers) **1.** He is referring to the unique
quality and traditional method of making each local product, like wine or
pecorino cheese. **2.** to enjoy life at a relaxed pace
After You Read: 1. A **2.** B **3.** C **4.** A **5.** B **6.** C **7.** B **8.** B **9.** A **10.** C
11. B **12.** D

Grammar Practice

Metaphors: A. 1. grasped **2.** starving **3.** weave **4.** pepper **B. 1.** sailed
2. road **3.** place **4.** journey

Hope vs. Wish: 1. Some people wish the festival happened twice a year.
2. The town hopes many tourists come for the festival. **3.** The children
wish they could have ice-cream every day.

Future Perfect Continuous: 1. will have been eating **2.** will have been
living **3.** will have been acting **4.** will have been running

Video Practice

A. 1. six **2.** 85 **3.** 1997 **B. 1.** along **2.** for **3.** on **C. 1.** ~~serving~~, creating
2. ~~seconds~~, minutes **3.** ~~the world~~, Europe **D. 1.** festival **2.** legend
3. battle **4.** particular **E. 1.** best **2.** pull **3.** almost **4.** helpless
F. 1. ~~southern~~, northern **2.** ~~over~~, across **3.** ~~interesting~~, dangerous
G. 1. ~~city~~, village **2.** ~~international~~, organised **3.** ~~condition~~, quality **4.** ~~500~~,
100 **H. 1.** days **2.** delightfully **3.** promotion **4.** life

Exit Test

1. C **2.** A **3.** 6 **4.** A **5.** B **6.** C **7.** D **8.** D **9.** T **10.** T **11.** D **12.** D **13.** C
14. B **15.** 10 **16.** A **17.** B **18.** A **19.** T **20.** F **21.** C **22.** A **23.** B **24.** A
25. D **26.** B **27.** C **28.** F **29.** T **30.** F

English - Chinese Vocabulary List 中英對照生詞表
(Arranged in alphabetical order)

Agatha Christie	阿嘉莎・克莉絲蒂	**inherently**	本質地
aggressive	好鬥的	**integrity**	完好無損
attire	服裝	**intrinsic**	內在的
be on to sth	想做某事	**Iron Curtain**	鐵幕
bland	枯燥乏味	**literal sense**	字面意思
boulevard	大街	**literary**	文學的
cherish	珍愛	**locomotive**	火車頭
cling to	緊貼	**lord**	領主
considerable	相當多	**lushness**	茂盛
constitute	構成	**maitre d'**	餐廳領班
desperately	非常努力地	**maniac**	狂熱份子
discreetly	謹慎地	**manifesto**	宣言
dominate	支配	**pamper**	呵護備至
epidemic	疫症	**parade**	炫耀
evolve into	慢慢演變	**passionate**	很熱愛
exotic	奇異的	**pop out**	突然離開
fighter jet	噴射戰鬥機	**practitioner**	參與者
furnishings	室內陳設	**presumptuous**	自以為是
hand mould	用手捏成某形狀	**prime**	最適合的
hang around	籠罩	**produce**	農產品
heavy bomber	巨型轟炸機	**quaint**	古色古香
homogenise	同質化	**resident**	居民

resolve	解決	thrilling	極刺激
soaked with	深受影響	travel compartment	火車車廂的隔間
spectator	觀眾	twist	扭曲變形
stand up to	經得起	undulating	起伏
stroll	漫步	venue	地點
superb	極好的	vet	審查
suspend	暫停	vine	葡萄
tension	拉緊的狀態	viniculture	釀製葡萄酒
terrain	地帶	visionaries	有遠見的人